For Maria, for everything

Text copyright © 2022 by Suzanne Lang
Cover art and interior illustrations copyright © 2022 by Max Lang

All rights reserved. Published in the United States by Random House Studio, an imprint of Random House Children's Books, a division of Penguin Random House LLC, New York.

Random House Studio with colophon is a trademark of Penguin Random House LLC.

GRUMPY MONKEY is a registered trademark of Pick & Flick Pictures, Inc.

Visit us on the Web! rhcbooks.com

Educators and librarians, for a variety of teaching tools, visit us at RHTeachersLibrarians.com

Library of Congress Cataloging-in-Publication Data is available upon request.
ISBN 978-0-593-48692-4 (trade) — ISBN 978-0-593-48693-1 (lib. bdg.) —
ISBN 978-0-593-48694-8 (ebook)

The text of this book is set in 18-point Bernhard Gothic.
Book design by Nicole Gastonguay

MANUFACTURED IN CHINA

10 9 8 7 6 5 4 3 2 1

First Edition

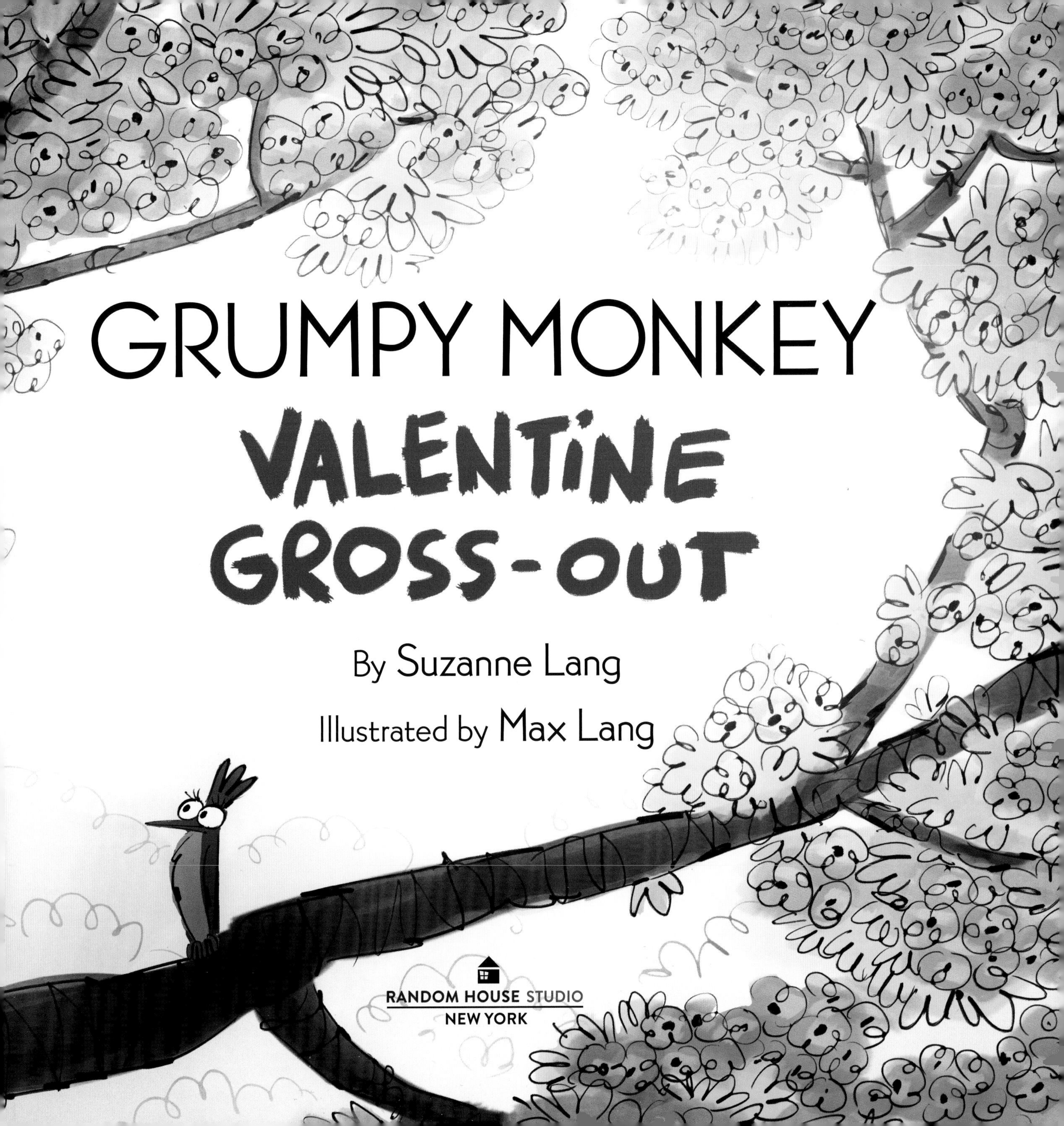

GRUMPY MONKEY
VALENTINE GROSS-OUT

By Suzanne Lang

Illustrated by Max Lang

RANDOM HOUSE STUDIO
NEW YORK

Jim Panzee was enjoying a nap in the sun when a voice awakened him.

"Jim! Do you like my flower?" tweeted Oxpecker. "My boyfriend gave it to me because we're in love!"

"Love!" said Jim. "Gross!"

"Don't be jealous! Also, my boyfriend is making me a romantic dinner for Valentine's Day," tweeted Oxpecker.

"Valentine's Day? What's that?"
asked Jim.

"It's a day for love," replied Oxpecker. "Full of hearts and sweets and flowers and romance. It's the lovey-est, dovey-est, most wonderful-est holiday!"

"Yuck," said Jim. "It sounds more like the grossest holiday!"

Jim went to find his neighbor Norman.
I bet Norman thinks Valentine's Day is as gross as I do, thought Jim.

But when he got to Norman's branch, his neighbor was busy.
"I'm making some love cards," said Norman. "Catch you later."
Jim couldn't believe it. Even Norman liked Valentine's Day!

Everywhere Jim went, there were couples being gross.

Couples exchanging cards.

Couples gazing into each other's eyes.

Couples giggling for no reason.

Couples slow-dancing.

Cuddling couples,

snuggling couples,

and, worst of all—kissing couples.

Finally, Jim couldn't take it anymore. "Ewww! Valentine's Day is the

GROSSEST HOLIDAY!"

"It's true—all the kissing is pretty gross," said Norman, "but Valentine's Day isn't just about couples.

"There are lots of kinds of love," said Norman. "Like the love you have for your parents."

"And the love parents feel for their children,"
said Jim's mom.

"And the love you feel for your friends," said Norman.

"Valentine's Day is about showing the people you love that you love them," said Jim's dad.

Jim's arms were full. Full of things that made him feel loved.
It was a nice feeling that he wanted to share.

And so he made valentines for all his friends and family.

Maybe Valentine's Day
isn't so gross after all,
he thought.